1P
92
#13⁹⁵

Let's go to the Museum

by **LISL WEIL**

Holiday House / New York

Library of Congress Cataloging-in-Publication Data

Weil, Lisl.
Let's go to the museum/written and illustrated by Lisl Weil.—
1st ed.
p.cm.
Summary: Explores different types of museums, tracing their
development from private collections to public exhibits and
describing directors, curators, trustees, conservators, public
relations people, and others who keep a museum running smoothly.
ISBN 0-8234-0784-5
1. Museums—History—Juvenile literature. 2. Museums—
Administration—Juvenile literature. 3. Museum techniques—
Juvenile literature. [1. Museums.] I. Title
AM7.W39   1989
069′.09—dc19   89-2078   CIP   AC

ISBN 0-8234-0784-5

Let's go to the
Museum

A visit to a museum is a journey into a marvelous wonderland. With our eyes, we can learn stories about the past or discover new things about the present or even the future. There are many different kinds of museums, but almost all of them focus on science, art, or history.

We can visit science and natural history museums and gaze at the skeletons of dinosaurs and other prehistoric animals that roamed the earth two hundred million years ago...

or we can go to art museums and look at beautiful paint-
ings and sculptures.

There are also museums that cover the history of a
nation, city, or town.

The house of a famous person who lived a long time ago sometimes becomes a museum that tells the history of that person's life.

PLANETARIUM

MUSEUM OF MODERN ART

FOLK·ART·MUSEUM

AMERICAN
ASIAN
AFRICAN
IRISH
INDIAN
JEWISH
GERMAN
AUSTRIAN
FRENCH
ITALIAN
POLISH
PUERTORICAN
SPANISH

UKRAINIAN · KOREAN · YUGOSLAVE · TIBETAN

1990

1910

MUSEUM of TRANSPORTATION

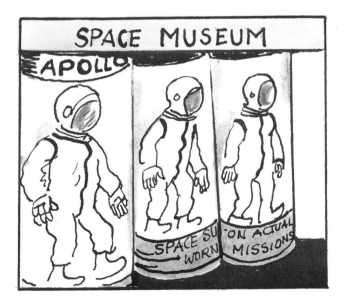

SPACE MUSEUM

APOLLO

SPACE SUITS WORN ON ACTUAL MISSIONS

AMERICAN INDIAN MUSEUM

Museums can have collections of almost anything—

COSTUME MUSEUM

BIBLE MUSEUM

SPORT MUSEUM

MANSION and MUSEUM

MUSEUM of the PERFORMING ARTS

POLICE·ACADEMY·MUSEUM

from planets to automobiles to costumes.

But museums have not always existed. Up until the third century B.C., there were no museums. People collected things privately instead.

PYRAMID: ANCIENT BURYING CHAMBER FOR ROYAL EGYPTIAN PRINCE

The ancient Egyptians of noble birth took their favorite jewelry, pets, toys, and other objects into their graves. They believed they would enjoy these things in the afterlife.

The first museum in the world is said to have been built by the ancient Greeks. In 307 B.C., Ptolemy Soter founded the "mouseion" in Alexandria, a Greek city in Egypt. It was built to honor the Muses, the nine goddesses who protected the arts and sciences. It included temples, gardens, a zoo, and a large library for scholars.

The word *museum* comes from the Greek word *mouseion*.

The ancient Romans were collectors, too. They conquered many nations and collected everything they could after a battle.

The Roman emperor Nero looted the cities and temples of Greece to decorate his house in Rome.

In the Middle Ages and the Renaissance, royal families in Europe and Russia collected beautiful objects for themselves. In Germany, they were kept in the *Schatzkammer* or treasury chamber. The treasures were admired only by the royal families.

Also during the Middle Ages, churches, monasteries, and universities had large private collections of rare manuscripts and religious art.

But it was the French Revolution in 1789 that led to museums as we know them today. The Revolution was fought by the poor and middle classes against King Louis XVI's court and the wealthy class. The common people felt that everyone, regardless of wealth, should be treated equally. When the war was over, the people of France demanded that private collections in palaces like the Louvre be open to the public.

In the nineteenth century, more and more collections in Europe became open to everybody.

American museums were planned for the public right from the start. Even though many wealthy Americans in the New World were fine private collectors, they often turned their collections over to larger museum collections when they died.

The first American museum was built in Charleston, South Carolina in 1773. It focused on the natural history of the region.

America's first art museum, originally the private collection of Charles Wilson Peale, a painter and inventor himself, opened in Philadelphia in 1784.

Boston's first museum was started in 1791 at the American Coffee House. It was an exhibit of wax figures that later became part of the New England Museum.

More than a third of the world's museums are in the United States!

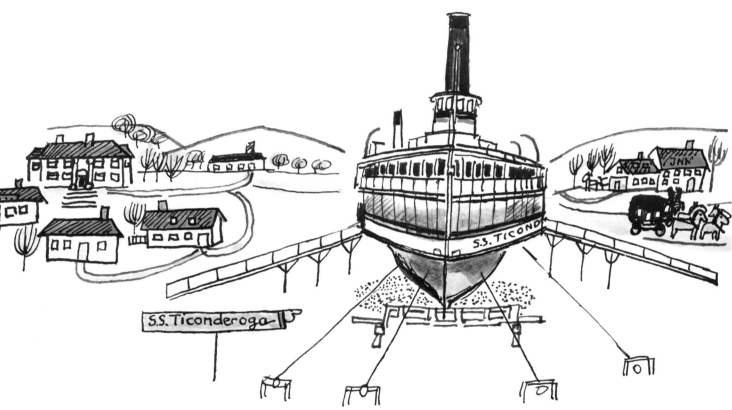

Today, we can also go to outdoor history museums. Several buildings and sometimes whole towns and cities form the museums. We can learn about the way people lived, built their homes, and worked during a particular period of history.

Children's museums are among the most popular of all museums. They usually have classrooms, libraries, and exhibits that help children learn more about the world around them.

The first children's museum in the United States was the Brooklyn Children's Museum. It was started in 1899.

The Children's Museum in Indianapolis is the largest children's museum in the world. It has a welcome center that has the world's tallest water clock as well as a "Passport to the World" gallery.

Museums are very busy places. Many people work hard to keep them running smoothly.

There is a director and a curator who plan the exhibits...and restorers and conservators who repair objects so that they'll look the way they used to.

Museums also have scouts who find treasures.

There are photographers to take pictures for researchers and for the catalog...and security guards to keep the treasures safe.

There are guides who point out facts about the exhibits to visitors. Sometimes, visitors listen to tapes that tell them more about the exhibits.

At the museum gift shop, one can shop for postcards, books and souvenirs to take home.

Most museums have rest rooms

and a place to get a snack, too.

Many museums have lecture halls, a first-aid station...and a coat-check area.

Museums often get very crowded. People may lose a pocketbook or a watch. Then they must go to Lost-and-Found.

Sometimes, famous museums send a few of their special treasures on a visiting tour to other grand museums —so more people everywhere may enjoy them.

Treasures are also donated to museums by governments and individuals.

Anything and everything has been collected by somebody, somewhere, at some time. From great masterpieces to cookie jars, all objects become a museum of our lives!

More about Museums

Here is a list of some different kinds of museums:

The Hermitage Museum in Leningrad, Russia was started by Peter the Great in 1714. It began as a private collection of coins and weapons.

ULYSSES S. GRANT

The American Museum of Natural History in New York was founded in 1869. Its cornerstone was laid in 1874 by President Ulysses S. Grant, the eighteenth president of the United States.

The Metropolitan Museum of Art was founded in 1870 by a group of wealthy New York industrialists and art collectors.

The Smithsonian Institution in Washington, D.C. was started in 1846 after the U.S. Government received a gift from English chemist James Smithson. Today, it is made up of separate museums that cover different areas of the arts, sciences, and history. Part of the Smithsonian, for example, is the National Air and Space Museum. Visitors can see Charles Lindbergh's famous plane, the *Spirit of St. Louis*, and the spaceship *Columbia*.

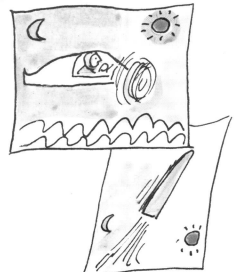

The John and Mable Ringling Museum of Art is in Sarasota, Florida. It grew out of circus owner John Ringling's private art collection. It has an art museum and the Museum of the Circus.

In Chicago's Museum of Science and Industry, visitors can walk inside a real German submarine captured during World War II.

The American Bible Society in New York City shows antique bibles, fragments of the Dead Sea Scrolls, and Braille volumes.

The old Cunard ocean liner, R.M.S. *Queen Mary*, has become a floating museum in Long Beach, California.

The Laura Ingalls Wilder Home and Museum is in Mansfield, Missouri. It honors the life of the author of *The Little House on the Prairie* books.

One of the best-known outdoor museums is Colonial Williamsburg. It has more than eighty buildings that have been restored to the way they looked in the eighteenth century.

Some of the most famous museums around the world are:

Louvre in Paris, France, which houses the famous painting *Mona Lisa* by Leonardo da Vinci.
Prado in Madrid, Spain
Uffizi Museum in Florence, Italy
British Museum, London, England
Museum of Modern Art, New York, New York

Index